The Beast of Bodmin Moor

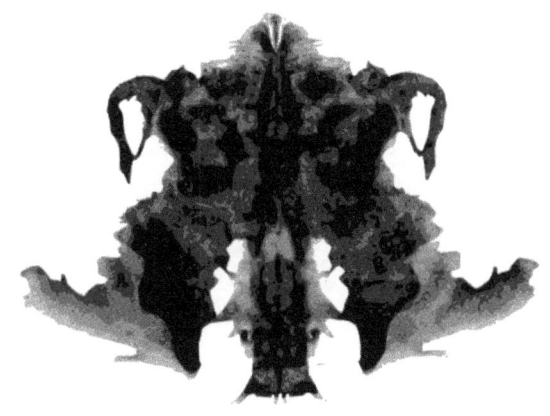

The Beast of Bodmin Moor

Nick Newitt

Green Rose Books
2019

Copyright © 2019 by Nick Newitt

All rights reserved. This book or any portion thereof may not be reproduced or used in any manner whatsoever without the express written permission of the publisher except for the use of brief quotations in a book review or scholarly journal.

First Printing: 2019

ISBN: 978 – 0 – 244 – 69357 – 2

Green Rose Books

www.green-rose.org

Dedication

To my amazing wife, Christine and my dearly beloved children and grandchildren: Tom, Katie, Lewis, Summer and Bella. Without your support and patience, I would be nothing.

To Becky, our very special daughter-in-law. Thank you for being a wonderful mother to our grandchildren. We love you like a daughter.

To my long-departed but never-forgotten mother, Wendy. You were a huge source of inspiration throughout my childhood. Mother. Artist. Role model. Friend. Thank you for introducing me to the works of Stephen King, James Herbert, Richard Laymon, Clive Barker and Dean Koontz.

To my father Roy. All my love.

Nick Newitt

The Beast of Bodmin Moor

It came from out of the darkness with the speed and deadly accuracy of a bullet. As flesh met flesh and claw met bone, the prone being knew that its life was soon to end. The beast ripped and slashed with intensity and passion, secure in the knowledge that as each second passed, the weaker of the two would die. Yet as its sharpness and voracity bit deep into the victim's flesh, there was a slowness, as if the creature was somehow relishing in the pain it was creating. And suddenly the victim's life ended. The beacon and strand of light between the soul and body was severed, beyond repair, and the creature of infinite evil drank in the bliss that was caused by the expiration of life. And death in the far beyond began; darkness and light mingled and wept, while time passed. The creature took its fill of the pleasures of cooling flesh.

*****

The Beast of Bodmin Moor

Evening Fred, nice to see you again. Cheers to you my brother. Merry Christmas to you as well! Here, sit down, have a drink on me. How have you been? Yeah. Yeah. Good. That sounds nice… look, I tell you what, come back to my house and we'll have a proper drink and catch up on all the gossip. Anyway, I have a good story to tell you; one which I have not told you before, and I am hoping it is one which you have not heard before. Come on then.

*****

Nick Newitt

The beast stomped through the forest with a purpose. It had not been seen, and it had engineered it so. With the blood of its fallen victim still clinging to the hairs about its face, it strode amongst the gnarled and broken trees towards its resting place near the river. The beast hated the feel of drying blood on its flesh; the way it clung and shrunk, and made the skin itch and tingle. The murder and subsequent violation of the latest victim incensed the creature to commit and recommit the same act, on different beings. It had observed, in the local village, a number of beings that deserved to be feasted upon. With subhuman thoughts, the creature made its plans against them.

For now though, it was time to rest. It laid down, in the cave which had once belonged to another predator, and slept. It dreamed dreams of murder: deep, dark sadistic dreams of torture and violence. And yet as it dreamt, it sensed a presence within the dreamworld. A voyager through the mind had somehow become entangled within the dream of the beast. In the world outside the dream, the beast snarled a toothy, evil grin.

*****

The Beast of Bodmin Moor

28th October 1993
The Diary of Mrs Davina Locker – Prophetess

Dear Diary,

Something has kept me awake all night, which I had presumed to be the spiritual world again. I wish that I had been wrong. What I saw disgusted me beyond belief.

At around two o'clock in the morning, something made me sit bolt upright in bed. Before my eyes came the familiar mix of auras which signalled the passage of the future into my present. From the colouring I could tell that evil was walking the earth again: black smoke tinged at the edges with purple swirled before me. In the centre however, there was a spark of white (purity) which tried to fight through the darkness, and shone with a brilliance brighter than the will of God.

Suddenly this haven of peace within the maelstrom collapsed, disintegrating and cycling through the colours of passion, lust, jealousy and finally, evil. This evil was darker than I have ever seen before. As I watched the colours imploded and the future picture became clear. The vision of degradation and violence

Nick Newitt

assaulted my eyes and they became spots of the most severe pain I have ever experienced. I saw snatches of life, as it will be. There was no evidence of hope in the images, just... death. I saw the vagina of a pregnant woman, her legs spread wide open. A baby's head forced its way out of her, and flopped onto the table. Within seconds the vision had twisted to that of The Beast. As it strode through a wheat field, it came upon a courting couple, enjoying the summer sun and each other's bodies. From where my spirit guide stood, I could see that the woman was pregnant, perhaps the same woman. The Beast dug its claws into the abdomen of the woman, and wrenched her off of the ground. With superhuman strength, it sliced her down the centre of her body, and dropped her failing flesh to the ground. The Beast reached down and picked up the foetus. It turned to the father of the child, and sneered. Opening its mouth wide, it held the foetus above its mouth and began to laugh. The Beast laughed with such ferocity that it was like an echo trembling within a hole as deep and cavernous as the centre of the Earth. It chilled my blood. The foetus fell into the maw of evil. The father attacked The Beast, but was killed instantly.

Suddenly the vision of the future ended, and although I did not want to see what was in store for the world, I

The Beast of Bodmin Moor

looked on, praying for a chance for change. It did not come. Instead, I switched from the spirit world to the dreamworld. And here my journey of terror truly began. I find it difficult to express my experiences, and yet I know now that I must.

The colours swirled and danced, tiny fairies and elves singing and screeching into the darkness of the night. The lights, darkness, fairies and elves imploded and I saw the dream in its entirety. I felt waves of pain rise up and crash down upon the reef of my despair. I saw The Beast inside this world of unconscious freedom walking down a road in the centre of the village. It was hairy, yet somehow naked: blood-red skin glistening in the darkness. Patches of the abomination's skin were black. Somehow I knew that this was human blood. The beautiful, rich blackness of blood when seen in the moonlight. I saw each globule, each plasma particle, as if I had been looking under a microscope, and I realized that murder was the object of desire for this demon.

Within the dream, I saw a river of blood flowing through the streets. It was a tidal wave of blood unleashed by the freak of nature. Bobbing upon the surface of this death wave, I saw the broken bodies of children, pensioners and middle-aged people alike. Even

Nick Newitt

though their corpses were defiled beyond recognition, I knew that they were my family, my friends, my lovers, my husband and myself. As I watched, my own eyeballs extracted themselves from the deluge of death and misery, and floated before me. I saw them, abstractly, as the cold lumps of jelly that they really are. I tried to twist my head away from the scene, but I was unable to move my sight from this dream-abomination.

Everywhere I looked I saw the same thing. No matter how much I tried, my eyes refused to close, and I was forced to look, to see, to know. Brown liquid oozed from the eyes in front of me that I recognised as my own, and as I stared fixedly at my own eyeballs in a state of slow disintegration, a scaly claw reached up, grabbed them and squeezed, squirting the viscous liquid all over me.

The tsunami of blood, guts, gore and babies crashed down upon me, then. It felt so real. I could smell the stench of rotting corpses. I could feel the weight of the bodies suffocating me. I also felt a pain in my chest. I looked down at my chest, and saw one of the Beast's claws embedded into it. Blood flowed freely from the wound. The aberration twisted and turned the claw,

The Beast of Bodmin Moor

slicing my heart into many pieces. At that point in the dream, I died, and my voyaging psyche was jettisoned into the real world. My hand shakes even as I try to relay this dream. I know that the village is in serious danger. I know that there is nothing that any of us can do. We are at the mercy of a slave of sadistic and evil dreams. The devil is amongst us, and we are in danger. Danger. May the Lord take pity on our souls.

*****

Nick Newitt

Fred, since you last came to visit, a lot of mysterious things have been happening in our village. I was under the misapprehension that the catastrophe had broken nationwide, but obviously not, as you say you haven't heard about it. Lucky for you then, that I kept a scrapbook of the newspaper articles concerning this terrible affair. As soon as the very first event occurred I knew that something awful was going to happen, but that there was nothing that we could do about it.

Make yourself at home, have a drink, a cigarette, anything. Thank you for sending me those matches a while back, it was very kind of you. Mrs Pettner often forgets her smoking clients and very rarely gets matches in. I don't know about you, but I can't stand those horrible lighter-things, you know. Anyway, as I say, make yourself at home, brother dear!

Would I like one of your cigarettes? Erm, yes, go on then, you can roll me one if you would be so kind. Cheers.

*****

The Beast of Bodmin Moor

This newspaper cutting shows the very first event which introduced what was soon to be called The Beast. On the whole, it went unnoticed, and many people just assumed that it was an attack made by a very hungry, vicious fox. Looking back with hindsight, everyone now agrees that it was The Beast. How could we have been so stupid as to think a whole flock of sheep could be mutilated and killed by a single fox? Even a <u>pack</u> of foxes could not have done that much damage, but that is what we thought it had to be.

We, well most of us, are churchgoers with strong religious backgrounds, so it was difficult to accept the supernatural even when, later, the facts were staring us in the face. Even now I find it difficult, and yet I know everything that happened. I must apologise if I do, from time to time, digress during this account, but please do forgive me my little outbursts. As I look back at all that has occurred I cannot help myself but think how stupid and blinkered our lives were. I am sorry, let me continue.

*****

Nick Newitt

Everyday is the same. Nothing changes, nothing interesting happens, and life goes on. We enjoy our lives, most of the time. Even if we do not appreciate the life we lead, there is nothing that we can do to change our future. People take away our children, and butcher them, yet we have no power. We are their cattle, their servants. We, the underlings of Man have no power, nor do we request it. We do not complain. No one would listen to us if we did. We exist, in and out of time. And yet, we are loved. We are loved by many, and betrayed by even more. We live at the perilous edge of their whims. As the tide changes, the moon rises, and the grass grows, we live and die. We live on the earth, and our blood is spilled upon the earth, to be regenerated, reused, reenergized and to give strength to humans. Sheep we are. Bitter, we are not. We exist, without these thoughts, yet they exist on our behalf: separate, yet joined by the subconscious efforts and emotions of sheephood.

We live, we eat, we die. But for now, we are safe, in a group. Togetherness is an important part of our lives. We have learnt through experience that isolation brings death. We are secure, and happy. The reason, of course, is that we are together and yet so alone.

As the flock of sheep grazed upon the grassy fields, these unspoken, unexpressed thoughts flowed through their minds. They were so caught up in their assumption of

The Beast of Bodmin Moor

security that they did not notice the black wretch stalking them. Instead of fleeing for their lives, as they surely should have done, the danger drew closer, and closer. With every passing second, the demon crept silently towards its prey.

And then, with a swift acknowledgement of their imminent death, the sheep saw The Beast. Before they even had time to consider reacting, the creature was upon them. They had seen humans taking one or two of their friends off to the slaughterhouse, but never had such a vile-looking bipedal being ever destroyed their kind with such ferocity and accuracy. With the cleaver-like claws of its massive paws, The Beast ripped each sheep apart, and the creature bathed in their blood and wore their entrails like medals; proof that it had power over every living thing in the country.

Leaving the field of sheep as a field of broken carcasses, the creature felt that he was stronger than the pull of the earth. He floated with the ambivalence and love of death and gore. Even though he loved the feel of flesh bursting and bending around his claws, the actual act of killing, of feeling the life-force leaving each victim's body, was near orgasmic; yet at the same time it was a disappointment, as the throes of death and pain and resistance ended too abruptly. The grotesque and indescribable evilness of The Beast forced it to keep killing, to keep the emotions

Nick Newitt

Everyday is the same. Nothing changes, nothing interesting happens, and life goes on. We enjoy our lives, most of the time. Even if we do not appreciate the life we lead, there is nothing that we can do to change our future. People take away our children, and butcher them, yet we have no power. We are their cattle, their servants. We, the underlings of Man have no power, nor do we request it. We do not complain. No one would listen to us if we did. We exist, in and out of time. And yet, we are loved. We are loved by many, and betrayed by even more. We live at the perilous edge of their whims. As the tide changes, the moon rises, and the grass grows, we live and die. We live on the earth, and our blood is spilled upon the earth, to be regenerated, reused, reenergized and to give strength to humans. Sheep we are. Bitter, we are not. We exist, without these thoughts, yet they exist on our behalf: separate, yet joined by the subconscious efforts and emotions of sheephood.

We live, we eat, we die. But for now, we are safe, in a group. Togetherness is an important part of our lives. We have learnt through experience that isolation brings death. We are secure, and happy. The reason, of course, is that we are together and yet so alone.

As the flock of sheep grazed upon the grassy fields, these unspoken, unexpressed thoughts flowed through their minds. They were so caught up in their assumption of

The Beast of Bodmin Moor

security that they did not notice the black wretch stalking them. Instead of fleeing for their lives, as they surely should have done, the danger drew closer, and closer. With every passing second, the demon crept silently towards its prey.

And then, with a swift acknowledgement of their imminent death, the sheep saw The Beast. Before they even had time to consider reacting, the creature was upon them. They had seen humans taking one or two of their friends off to the slaughterhouse, but never had such a vile-looking bipedal being ever destroyed their kind with such ferocity and accuracy. With the cleaver-like claws of its massive paws, The Beast ripped each sheep apart, and the creature bathed in their blood and wore their entrails like medals; proof that it had power over every living thing in the country.

Leaving the field of sheep as a field of broken carcasses, the creature felt that he was stronger than the pull of the earth. He floated with the ambivalence and love of death and gore. Even though he loved the feel of flesh bursting and bending around his claws, the actual act of killing, of feeling the life-force leaving each victim's body, was near orgasmic; yet at the same time it was a disappointment, as the throes of death and pain and resistance ended too abruptly. The grotesque and indescribable evilness of The Beast forced it to keep killing, to keep the emotions rearing their ugly head, to keep the death game alive. As it destroyed more and more beings, its power and strength grew in immeasurable amounts, and its lust for blood, killing and death became vastly unsated.

*****

The Beast of Bodmin Moor

It should come as no surprise to you, then, that as each killing spree occurred, the Beast destroyed more and more sheep. After a while, the Beast seemed to grow unsatisfied with sheep, and moved on to humans. Once it had tasted human blood, it never went back to the animal kingdom. From that point, no human was safe to go out alone.

Admittedly, the Beast began slowly, taking only one human every few days or so. Eventually the thirst for killing must have become too much for it, and it descended upon our village with increasing intensity. On the 19th June of last year, the bodies of three friends were discovered. They were only children. Well, teenagers who thought that they were adults, but really they were just children! My God, children. I am sorry, but why would anything want to hurt children? It was then that I began to think that maybe this creature was really an emissary from Satan.

When I discussed it with Father O'Shea, he convinced me that it was simply a beast of the forest, intent only on feeding, and protection. The children, he explained, were out at a time when badgers and the like were hungry, and had families of their own to protect, and that the children must have invaded the privacy of the animals of the

Nick Newitt

forest. I found this hard to believe, but accepted his word as a priest. I had faith in him. I truly believed that I had no reason to disbelieve him, but in the end it was the facts of the case which took over from ideological uncertainties.

What happened to them? As the story goes,

> **The Bodmin Bugle**　　　　　　**20 June**
>
> **Bodmin Children Slaughtered**
>
> Kieran, James and Winnifred Mulwinney were brutally murdered late last night. As they walked home from their uncle's house, they were set upon viciously and without conscience. As they walked along the narrow path beside the park, in single file, each child was dragged soundlessly from the line and subsequently butchered.
>
> Police Constable Davidson believes that these "unfortunate children" could be victims of what this newspaper has termed "The Beast". He intends to request support from local constabularies so that a thorough search can be made for The Beast, and so that it can be destroyed. It must not be forgotten, though, that three children have died, and those who wish to pay their

The Beast of Bodmin Moor

> respects to the family are welcome to attend the funeral which will be held at St Benedict's Church on Wednesday.

Of course I went to the funeral and paid my respects to the childrens' parents, but even as I spoke to them, I felt the emptiness of my words. How could my clichèd responses to these deaths ever fill the gulf that must exist within Mr and Mrs Mulwinney's hearts? I gave up, realising the feebleness of my attempts. It was the first funeral I had been to in this village, and it was destined not to be my last, for soon afterwards The Beast struck again. A courting couple went to the local cinema, the ABC on 29th June and saw an adult movie. Thus incensed with passion it is said, they moved on to the park.

*****

Nick Newitt

They were invisible to the world. Their bodies were separate, yet seemingly joined at the soul. They knew the world was wrapped around them, yet they saw, heard and smelt nothing but each other. Similarly, entwined within themselves, they became fleshless. By exposing their wanton flesh, the world looked on and saw nothing.

They were strangers in a strange land, exploring uncharted territories of ecstasy and eroticism. Two lovers searching, probing, taking pleasure from the other's body.

They met. They fell into lust. They sought the utopic arena of intercourse. A young girl and a young man, both desperate to fulfil their own individual sexual desires, yet still desiring seduction, eroticism and uncontrolled ecstasy.

Once at the park bench, after a long journey, they quickly and ravenously removed their clothing. They stood before each other, bathing in the beauty of the toned and curved bodies reflecting the dying sun, the falling of the day.

As the flowers lay down to sleep, the young man laid on the park bench, his phallus pointing at the moon. The young girl took the iron-hard member in her hand, marvelling at the texture and heat it produced within her hand. Slipping the engorged, purple head between her lips, she turned around so that her genitals were above his

The Beast of Bodmin Moor

mouth. As she sucked and licked him to a point of near climax, he slid his tongue into the very entrance of her vagina; his nose nuzzling her tingling flesh. His bottom lip massaged the extended clitoris and his tongue probed further inside her. He felt a pressure inside, and realised that the young girl was a virgin. He found it difficult to believe.

She had pulled his throbbing, hard, hot penis deep inside her mouth, the size of it almost making her gag. However, like a circus sword eater she let it slide down her throat entrance. Her tongue flickered over, and played around his penile column, while her lip muscles massaged the base of it. He was swiftly approaching climax, and felt her vagina tighten around his tongue. He slowed and quickened his licks and teases, in an attempt to force a simultaneous orgasm. He succeeded, and both of their writhing, naked bodies began to shudder and gulp. The beautiful young girl swallowed the young man's semen, and licked her lips with glee.

Before he could soften, she turned herself around and slowly and painfully impaled her virginal sex upon his manhood. As she rode up and down him, she noticed the audience around her. In bushes surrounding them were birds, cats and dogs. She did not care. She saw them yet did not see. They became part of the eroticism, enhanced the ecstasy.

Nick Newitt

Both orgasmed again, the girl's large breasts swaying back and forth, nipples erect and red. She climbed off, dressed, kissed him on the nipple and left. The man laid back, still naked and solidly erect, and smiled. With trembling hands, he lit a cigarette, one of the many that he had rolled earlier that evening, and took long, deep drags from it. The deep aroma and texture of the smoke entranced him, and he sucked greedily upon the weed. He looked all around him, not embarrassed in the slightest that he was naked in public, and marvelled at how quiet and peaceful it was there.

From out of the bushes beside him flashed a deep, blood red light. Turning his head slightly, he looked straight into two red eyes. The Beast. Before he could register shock, huge claws began their butchery upon him, slitting his body from one end to the other. With an accuracy and sharpness equalled only by surgeons, the crude autopsy was carried out. The voyeurs to sex became witnesses to death. Each one died, in turn. Whether through beast or shock, they died. The Beast knew they were there, had allotted a time for their death.

The butchery would soon be over for this one, poor wretched soul, but for now it continued with the savage remains of spiteful hatred towards everything human. When it had finished, the unlawful issue of evil had left

The Beast of Bodmin Moor

the park and the bench swimming in a pool of sticky, sickly blood.

*****

Nick Newitt

Both orgasmed again, the girl's large breasts swaying back and forth, nipples erect and red. She climbed off, dressed, kissed him on the nipple and left. The man laid back, still naked and solidly erect, and smiled. With trembling hands, he lit a cigarette, one of the many that he had rolled earlier that evening, and took long, deep drags from it. The deep aroma and texture of the smoke entranced him, and he sucked greedily upon the weed. He looked all around him, not embarrassed in the slightest that he was naked in public, and marvelled at how quiet and peaceful it was there.

From out of the bushes beside him flashed a deep, blood red light. Turning his head slightly, he looked straight into two red eyes. The Beast. Before he could register shock, huge claws began their butchery upon him, slitting his body from one end to the other. With an accuracy and sharpness equalled only by surgeons, the crude autopsy was carried out. The voyeurs to sex became witnesses to death. Each one died, in turn. Whether through beast or shock, they died. The Beast knew they were there, had allotted a time for their death.

The butchery would soon be over for this one, poor wretched soul, but for now it continued with the savage remains of spiteful hatred towards everything human. When it had finished, the unlawful issue of evil had left

The Beast of Bodmin Moor

the park and the bench swimming in a pool of sticky, sickly blood.

*****

Nick Newitt

The Bodmin Bugle   **31 July**

Proof Found Of Beast's Existence

Forensic Scientists at the sight of last night's mauling, which involved the Right Honourable Kenneth Bluegrieb, have announced a very important finding. When they moved Bodmin Moor's Member of Parliament, they found a large, unexplained pawprint on the ground. It seems that from the depth and size of the prints, the creature weighs over 20 lbs, and is approximately 7ft in height. Questions were raised at the Press Conference where this information was disclosed, asking why there was only one pawprint, however police spokespeople were unwilling to speculate.

One suggestion made by Leon Odie, head of the Forensic Research Team, is that the rains of the following evening may have washed away the other prints, and that this one print was preserved due to the fact that Mr Bluegrieb's body had fallen onto it.

We at The Bugle feel that this proves, once again, our theories that The Beast is truly an entity and not simply the "product of

The Beast of Bodmin Moor

overworked minds" as Detective Inspector John Bayliss has previously asserted.

*****

Nick Newitt

Overworked minds! Although news did break nationwide that there was a reputed Beast in Bodmin Moor, it was not known of the extent to which proof had been found. Many people in the rest of the country, as National newspapers proved, thought that The Beast was just a hoax to increase tourism. I dare say that before I started telling you this story, you believed the same. That is the power that the media have over the thought processes of the world population.

Even though the existence of the pawprint was shown not to be a fake, many people even in this village had their doubts. These were soon to be crushed.

Summer had turned into Autumn, and the crispness of the season was making itself known. The Fourth of September arrived, and the Beast who had not exactly been dormant, but had indeed slowed its death toll considerably, reawoke.

*****

The Beast of Bodmin Moor

Jack Kerry was the Editor of The Bodmin Bugle. How he came to Bodmin Moor was hidden behind a mask of professionalism and a strong moral code. He knew the truth behind the lies, but no other living soul in that part of the country did. They had welcomed him with open arms.

The truth was that before being forced out of his job, he was a two-bit reporter for the London Chronicle. Although many crimes occurred in London, Jack was not satisfied. He wanted to report on crimes as lurid and exciting as they could possibly be, but instead he was constantly sent out to report on what he considered to be boring stories. He felt the need to create a web of deceit which involved the rather glamorous and bebauched lifestyle of famous rock star, Thorn – the lead singer from Golgotha. Instead of telling the truth concerning the rock star's life, Jack created a slew of newsworthy reports, which painted Thorn as a child-molesting "demon" who preyed on small boys. No matter how Thorn denied the lies, Jack was ready with another story, parading "evidence" his investigation claimed to have unearthed. Jack littered the pages of the London Chronicle with photographs of liaisons with sex-trafficked children and his personal security guards. The so-called evidence was expertly manufactured by a dear friend of his, but when Jack Kerry and the London Chronicle were sued for libel, Thorn won convincingly. The court were shown how Jack

Nick Newitt

had commissioned these photographs, and his solicitors proved that they were inaccurate by asking Thorn to remove his shirt and tie. On the photographs, the image showed "Thorn" with the tattoo of an anchor on his right arm. Thorn did not have any tattoos, as any legitimate rock photographer could have told him. In his pursuit for a juicy story, Jack had failed to carry out any effective research.

The people of Bodmin Moor were uninterested in the lives and loves of rock stars, so they did not know Jack Kerry's involvement with the scandal. They did not even know of the scandal itself. They led a cloistered life, which concerned only each other. Jack Kerry blended in very well, and soon became the Editor of The Bodmin Bugle.

Sitting in his office on the fourth of September, he examined his awards; for reporting excellence. He looked at the trophy he had received following publication of the Thorn Report and smiled a bitter-sweet smile. He was not remorseful in the slightest, and he loved the award. It was made of ebony, yet it shone with a golden gleam.

He was up very late tonight, as he was writing a report which concerned, yet again, The Beast. It was a cleverly written piece, which used symbolism of the Devil, and described the crimes it had committed as an "insult to the

The Beast of Bodmin Moor

majesty of God", whom he secretly despised. He was not interested in hypocrisy. He just hoped that people would read his newspapers and be horrified by the events that he described.

Jack sat back in his chair with a smug grin on his face, and stubbed out his cigarette. He looked at the wall clock, which read ten minutes to two o'clock in the morning, and he felt that he must be hallucinating. This egocentric man, who had no qualms about ruining any human being's career, saw the hands of the clock curl upwards. They appeared to look like horns. The centerpiece began to pull and twist the clock face until it looked like a snout. Jack Kerry watched with surprised interest at this hallucination, not daring to look away or blink, for fear that it would disappear. The clock had changed from a flat piece of cheap plastic into what looked like a three-dimensional face of a dog, with horns.

Jack felt drunk; happy, yet confused. Never taking his eyes from the mysterious transformation, he stood up to take a closer look at this strange phenomenon. As he did so however, the white plastic turned into a deep, blood-red colour and became very hairy. Jack was extremely scared, especially considering that no alcohol had passed his lips for over three days. He attempted to convince himself that this was simply a bad dream caused by the stress of having to work so hard to meet print deadlines, but when the clock face actually spoke, he fell down and sunk deeper into his armchair. In a voice that sounded slightly metallic, and in a tone of utter disgust, the clock-snout shouted deeply offensive obscenities. When it had completed this unholy prayer of degradation, it paused as if to take breath. It spoke again.

"You dare to mock my unholy name? You dare to write such lies about me, the most influential and evil entity in the mythology of your world? You call me an abomination of the sacrificial union between a priest and a whore, and do not expect me to defend myself?" it said.

As it was speaking, Jack noticed that the clock was beginning to stretch once again. The thin, weak plastic of the clock stretched and stretched until the whole, wretched body of the being which proclaimed itself to be Satan could be seen. The blood-red creature of infinite evil and pain was thus suspended perpendicular to the wall, as if it had been glued by its cloven hooves to the surface. The creature, now fully extended from the wall, began to tear and strip away the plastic which encased it. As Jack watched in horrified awe, he saw the true form of The Beast. The creature disappeared with an abruptness equalled only by Prima Ballerinas, whom Jack would indulge in upsetting, for the sheer pleasure of seeing their controlled, yet unsurpassed rage.

The Beast of Bodmin Moor

Jack was alone, and yet he felt as though he were being watched with cold, deadly eyes, whose hatred and forceful animosity were centred deep upon his own darkly wretched soul. Jack suddenly focused his senses on the vile stench of death and old, depraved sexual conduct. The deep, evil breath seemed to issue from behind him. He could feel the warmth of this breath on the back of his neck, and realised with the clarity of pure diamonds that The Beast stood behind him. He turned, and sat nose-to-nose with the snout of evil breathing up his nostrils. Close up the stench of death was stronger, so strong that as he accidentally inhaled deeply, he felt as though he would gag.

Opening its mouth slightly, Jack was shown the multifaceted, dual-rowed curved teeth which lined the inside of the destructive being's maw. Unable to remove his sight from the face, Jack looked into the pools of light that humans would mistakenly have called eyes. Instead of glistening balls of jelly, The Beast was in possession of pools of fire. As the creature stared deep into Jack's own eyes, the fire seemed to grow and burn with the intensity of Hell. As he tried to turn his head yet again, the creature fastened a talon-filled, almost human paw around his cheeks, and dug in those blood-tinged claws. Despite the pain and desire for escape, Jack was forced to look again at the eyes of the demon. The fire grew and shone, and eventually it was so large that it consumed all that Jack could see. The red tongues of fire did indeed come from Hell, and so too did the visions that he was forced to watch. For his own, private pleasure, Jack saw each mutilation and murder. Past his eyes flew the faces of those victims who had died painfully and savagely; the sheep, the children, the lovers, himself. Too shocked to react, he realised that he had seen too much. As The Beast had been replaying, through the fires for Jack, the many murders and butchery that had occurred, the creature had shown a weakness. He had shown Jack too much, or was it intentional?

Before he had a chance to move, the demon had disappeared again. Jack spun around, convinced that it would still be there, but it was not. It had gone. He was alone.

He grabbed the handle of his phone, put it to his ear and was about to dial a number – it did not matter who – when he heard a deep-throated chuckle. It was such an evil, malicious laugh that Jack did not for one second mistake it. The Beast. It spoke again:

"You must die, Jack Kerry. Your reign of scandal, your web of lies must end, and believe it or believe it not, you will not be missed. I showed you part of my intentions for your sexually perverse, disgusting little vomit-scented body, but not all. I held back my most inventive of

The Beast of Bodmin Moor

intentions. Before your life force is snuffed out, I will rip that lying, mischievous tongue from that festering tar pit of a mouth of yours. I will without any hesitation break all of the fingers from your hands. I, the Prince of Darkness, do not wish you to bring your lies with you to Hell. Once you die, you will suffer the most mind-blowing, torturous eternity ever conceived by my minions. Do you feel remorse, you pestilential, pitiful excuse for a man?"

Before Jack could reply, the creature had reappeared before him. With the swiftness and deadliness of a snake, The Beast of Evil struck.

*****

Nick Newitt

His secretary, June Bradfield, found his corpse the next morning. She, as you can imagine was deeply shocked and extremely horrified. Shortly after finding what was left of his body, she left the village. I just can not understand why The Beast found it necessary to kill a harmless newspaper editor. Even when his Editorial about The Beast was published after he died, I could not understand it. But then, all of the people that The Beast destroyed were kind, generous people, who loved life and lived it to the full. Hell, you could have quite easily been a victim; anyone in this village could have been. I nearly was, but I will come back to that later.

*****

The Beast of Bodmin Moor

After the death of Jack Kerry there was a great, public demonstration on the Village Green, on the seventh of October. People from all over Bodmin came to it. They knew that The Beast's activities centred around our quiet village, and were unhappy about how the case was being dealt with. No one had faith in the authorities. I mean, over twenty people had died, and the police were no closer to finding the awful creature responsible now, than they had been at the start.

*****

Nick Newitt

The Bodmin Bugle   **23 October**

Sign Of The Devil

A strange, unexplained phenomenon occurred late last night, as the sun fell out of the sky, which led onlookers to jump to conclusions. Mr Alfred Peterson, 85, who is a member of the Bodmin Paranormals, said that the blood-red colour of the sky was a "portent from Satan". Allegedly, as he and his friends watched, the clouds shifted and formed a more "potent warning of Satan's power" – a set of three sixes.

*****

The Beast of Bodmin Moor

I was very afraid, as was the whole village. I am not normally superstitious, but I noticed that the air seemed to crackle with an unspoken expectation of death. That night, almost all of the village locked themselves into their own homes. Six people thought it safe to walk across the village to their relatives' homes. Six people died. It was then that myself and the majority of the village believed fully in The Beast as an evil entity.

Before, we could just imagine it being an errant, vicious zoo animal, but with the portents and omens we had no choice but to cast aside our assumptions and accept the frightening reality.

And then, Jack Kerry spoke from the grave, in an Editorial he had started to write before he had died. With all the funeral arrangements it had somehow been lost, and then – before hardly any time had passed at all, a dead man spoke. I do apologise if you consider me to be a tad callous, but I find it distasteful to print a dead man's work so soon after his death.

*****

Nick Newitt

The Bodmin Bugle   25 October

Last Editorial Of Jack Kerry

A lot of my readers have written to me explaining in great detail their theories that the Beast of Bodmin Moor is not a wild zoo animal as I have suggested in the past, but an emissary of the devil intent upon reaping our souls. While you are entitled to your own views, I would ask you not to send such pompous letters based on circumstantial evidence.

I have a theory of my own. I do not believe that there is a Beast at all, but that a serial killer is living in the village…

And it goes on. I was quite willing to believe it until the information concerning his scandal arose in the village. Once the national media found out that Jack "Web of Lies" Kerry, as they dubbed him, had died, certain newspapers sent various replicas of old scandals, which rubbished everything that he had ever said. The village soon saw the "wonderful" Jack Kerry as a beast, himself.

*****

The Beast of Bodmin Moor

I myself saw The Beast, you know. It happened shortly after the Editorial was published. I was walking down Pulley Park Road late at night. I suppose I was stupid to be out at night when The Beast was probably on the prowl, but I took great exception to having to lock myself away in my lonely cottage. As I walked along I kept hearing rustling noises in the bushes, which frightened me intensely. With great determination I ignored these noises, hoping it was nothing. Then, almost as if I had developed a sixth sense, I looked around. My blood curdled at what I saw: The Beast.

It was crouched down, as if ready to strike, but when it saw me looking, it pulled itself up to its full height. Believe me when I tell you that it seemed to tower above the trees. It was covered from head to foot with a form of brown fur, which gave it the impression of being a pussy cat. Yet, even from that distance I saw the white maggots wriggling about. What I had first assumed was the wind moving and rustling its fur, was really the excited mating dance of a thousand larvae.

Here and there upon its body were bald patches, where the furry substance seemed to have been ripped out. In its place were deep, festering wounds which seemed to travel from its head. The head was a very frightening sight, what with its dog-like snout and vampiric teeth. Yet despite its animalistic features it seemed to grin with human characteristics. It showed me its razor-pointed fangs, and as it did so it began to drool a deep-red substance.

My sight moved up and stared right into the beacons of fire which seemed to be set like jewels into its head. These eyes were pools of evil, which seemed to bore deep into me, as if searching for my soul. I felt a twang deep within me, as my soul was pulled slowly but surely from my body. And then, suddenly it seemed to rush back inwards.

The Beast's dog-like ears pricked up, as if it had heard something, and with the speed at which it had seemed to appear, it was gone. I was saved.

You may be wondering how I can remember these details so vividly, when I had only seen it for less than a minute. Until my dying day, the sight of The Beast standing before me that night will remain with me. As those hellish eyes bore into my soul, those images were burned into my mind.

I was lucky. There were others who were not so lucky.

The Beast of Bodmin Moor

*****

Nick Newitt

It came from out of the darkness, with a speed paralleled only, in the animal kingdom, by a cheetah. It was as swift, yet ultimately more deadly. It brought down its victims faster and with greater efficiency. As The Beast stalked and sprang through the forest, seizing the human prey by throat and chest, it made sure that once they were down, they never stood up again. It loved the resistance that each victim, regardless of their gender or age, gave. Each lower being fought against the power and sadism of The Beast. Each one was forced to accept their failure when their breathing was cut short, and their tiny hearts stopped.

The Beast looked into the eyes of one of the women, and saw a tear forming. It dropped from her eyes and fell onto The Beast's arm. Its physical effect was to sting like battery acid, yet it had a more profound effect upon The Beast's mind.

It lifted up the body of that woman, as if offering it up to the glories of Heaven, and then it ripped and slashed with an intensity that shocked even itself. Visibly shaken at its own ferocity, it stepped back. The Beast sat down among the ruined and wretched, torn corpses and somehow tried to make sense of what had happened. Deep within the psyche of The Beast, it had felt a spasm of remorse, a spasm which had echoed throughout the muscular and mental definition of its being, and it had metamorphosed

The Beast of Bodmin Moor

that remorse into the pursuit of malicious intent. The vibrancy of this highly enhanced new self-perception was intoxicating.

Forcing itself to regain control, and secure once more within its own psyche, it left those half-mutilated corpses and ran into a field of cows. He summoned this new strength and rage and slaughtered the entire herd. It drank upon the cattle's blood and ate the entrails that hung in and around their bodies. Feeling refreshed after consuming this cocktail of gore, it ran back to the resting place it had secured a long time ago.

The Beast took time to reflect upon recent events, and found itself to be confused. Why had it not attacked the human near the Park? It had been busy ripping out the soul of the human, when it had heard a call from the forest. With the acute hearing it had been created with, it had observed the presence of the camping tourists, and knew what had to be done. This puny male of the wretched species was covered with layers of grime which equaled its years. His blood was impure and infertile for The Beast's evil purpose. These humans in this village were destined for a wider, more malevolent purpose. Their blood belonged to The Beast. Their entrails would be decorations upon the walls of its anger. Nothing in this pitiful world could stop it, nor could it ever wish to try.

Nick Newitt

*****

The Beast of Bodmin Moor

The Bodmin Bugle   29 October

Forensic Report

Forensic scientists and analysts have found an "unknown substance" in the tobacco of the man murdered on the 29th June. More tests are needed, but it is suspected that the substance could be a rare form of cannabis.

I almost missed that tiny article, but I kept it, perhaps as if I had had a premonition of things to come.

*****

Nick Newitt

Later on in the week my neighbour, Mrs Davina Locker… died. She was alone in the dead of night, and it is rumoured that she was murdered by a burglar. Some people in the village believe that it was The Beast.

You may laugh, Fred, but at that time in the village, every crime that involved mutilation or death – and there were many, believe me – was thought to have been brought about by The Beast. Obsession, you <u>may</u> call it, but I am simply explaining what happened.

She was a lovely woman. It was a damn shame, if you pardon my language, that she died at all, never mind at the hands of a burglar.

*****

The Beast of Bodmin Moor

The dream voyager. The Beast knew with deadly conviction that once a being knows of your power or intentions, it can change the course of the future. With an evil and malicious greed for killing, it knew that the woman had to die. The Beast stalked through the house with an animalistic silence. It sniffed the air, searching for the scent of perfume that it had detected in the remnants of its dream. It found her. It slayed her. It ripped her. It carved her. It reduced her to a smear of crimson pulp.

Davina Locker bled, but not before she had seen the true, non-dream-induced nightmarish vision of The Beast she had witnessed previously. As it approached her, she screamed part of a word which meant nothing to anyone but herself and The Beast: "child". The Beast knew of her children. The dream had shown the lambs, ready for The Slaughter.

*****

Derek Wagstaff was a strange man. He was a self-confessed paranormal investigator. Over the thirty three years of his career he had searched out ghosts, ghouls and many other types of strange ectoplasmic phenomena. He had uncovered many hoaxes and upset a great many people. He felt no shame at dragging up memories of dead relatives in his search for the truth. Mysteries, he often explained, were there simply to be solved. Behind every mystery was a perfectly scientifically provable explanation. The reasons he gave to clients for ghostly visitations ranged from echoes of a past era caught up in the genetic matrices of bricks in a room, combined with increasing temperatures or o-zone depletion…to pure and simple hoaxes by "haunted house" owners looking to tap into the paranormal tourism market. Although he never actually managed to convince anyone that his opinions were the truth, he tried hard.

He had heard about The Beast of Bodmin Moor, and the various theories that were revolving the Paranormal Invetigation World, by reading the Journal of Paranormal Activity. He intended to find out the truth.

Derek had arrived in Bodmin Moor unprepared. He had remembered to bring his scientific equipment, but had forgotten the bare essentials: food and tobacco.

The Beast of Bodmin Moor

He went into the local grocer-come-tobacconist shop, Mrs Pettner's, and bought enough food for a week, and enough tobacco for a fortnight. From there he took all of his equipment to the forest, and set up his camouflaged shelter. He sat in the dark, with his night-vision binoculars on and waited.

He waited for almost an hour and nothing came. He rolled up a cigarette and as he smoked it he listened for any signs of the elusive Beast. He heard and saw nothing other than the almost silent whirrs and clicks of his equipment.

The Beast leapt and landed in front of Derek's shelter. It had seen a light through the trees and knew that it had to investigate. Derek crawled out of his shelter, not yet realising the danger that was in front of him. As he stood up he felt slightly light-headed and woozy. Instead of the ferocious monster he had heard so much about in the Journal, he simply saw a hairy man. As his mind tried to understand what his eyes were seeing, Derek realised his mistake. He found himself being dragged back into the shelter.

No matter how much he screamed and shouted, and kicked at the creature whose power he was under, he could not move it. Just as he could not move a mountain, so Derek was unable to pry the creature's grip from his body. He was powerless and completely at the mercy of The Beast.

Derek screamed and screamed in anguish and although his pleas could be heard throughout the village, no one there was stupid enough to rush to his aid. The Beast tore at him with claws the strength of steel, and as his flesh parted and his life faded, Derek wished that he had brought a gun.

He had expected to come to Bodmin and uncover a hoax of enormous proportions. He had not expected to come across a demon of this caliber. His body was eventually spread over an area the size of a kilometer, and his blood mingled with the waters of the river he had camped beside. This time, at least, The Beast did not have far to go to rest.

*****

The Beast of Bodmin Moor

All in all, that night was a good hunt for The Beast. Eleven stupid tourists camped in the forest, and as this article proves, they all died:

The Bodmin Bugle   30 November

Eleven Fall Foul Of The Beast

With what has now become a depressing frequency, The Beast has struck again. Eleven people: men, women and children, were in their own private small groups, camped in the forest. These tourists did not know any better, and in the pursuit of a happy holiday, they have been brutally slain. The Bugle's sympathy goes to the families of the victims, and the time is long overdue for a public, official enquiry. It is known that police have carried out "private investigations", however they have, as yet, not been able to uncover any proof of The Beast's existence. Once again, the response from authorities is "no comment". So, while our village lives in daily and nightly fear, the hands of those employed to protect us are "tied". May God save our souls!

*****

The extent of our fear at this time, and even now, was indescribable. Even though many of us had turned away from God, we did find our way back, for a reason. We wanted a macrocosmic answer. We wanted to know why God was turning his back on our pleas for help. Why was he torturing us, and destroying our lives? Do you know what answer we were given by Father O'Shea? Do you?

In one of his sermons, he went on at great length about how Satan was involved. His language was appalling – he was effing and blinding everywhere. We presumed that he had been indulging in the communion wine a tad too much, however this did not answer our questions. We knew that The Beast was a form of demon sent to torment us, but we wanted to know why God had forsaken us. Were we, the survivors, intended for a greater purpose as His own forsaken Son had been? Were we heck!

*****

The Beast of Bodmin Moor

Father Stephen O'Shea took one last swig of his Famous Grouse, and stubbed out his cigarette. He had sat up nearly all night writing a sermon for the following day's mass. Now, after only three hours of sleep, he felt an urge to practice this scathing sermon, in situ, so to speak.

Father Stephen was the only priest who had access to the keys which let him into the chapel, and now and then he liked to practice. "Practice will ultimately always lead to perfection," his mother had always told him, so whenever the opportunity arose, he practiced. His sermons were always long, and always scathing, however just recently his sermons seemed to be attacks upon the devil and the emissary of evil, The Beast. Most of his congregation completely believed that The Beast was "from Hell", so Stephen used it to his full advantage. In his own way, Stephen O'Shea was a megalomaniac, and he loved nothing more than scaring people into church. The greater the fear, the bigger the congregation – the more swollen the collection, the finer the wine. As he orated, he felt strength and power flow into him, as his words flowed out. He felt as if he were greater and more powerful than the combined efforts of God and Satan themselves.

Stephen had very interesting views about Satan, considering that he was a priest. He truly believed that Satan was nothing but a tool of the Church. He thought that the Church used the imagery of a demonic creature to recruit converts. Whenever he was low on ideas for a sermon, he brought out the devil, and blamed him for all kinds of problems within society: alcohol, abortion, contraception, general and specific fornication, etc.

He stood at the lectern feeling the wood shift around his eminently strong and powerful hands. He looked into the dark and empty pews. He imagined the flock of impressionable sheep, begging him to speak; aching for him to sermonise. They milked his every syllable. They loved and adored him. They wanted to hear what his views were on today's subject:

"Ladies and gentlemen, I am afraid that I have not had time to compose this sermon in advance, so I ask you to bear with me if I lose my thread. [PAUSE] The devil. The bane of society. Even as you sit here, listening to me, the devil is walking, nay slithering across the earth. He is fornicating with your daughters, buggering your sons and forcing alcohol down the throats of your unemployed friends. This monster is responsible for the millions of teenage pregnancies, for abortion, for contraception, for stillborn children, war, famine, pestilence and death, and for the handicapped. As perfectly normal babies are inside their mother's womb, the devil is twisting them, and turning their bodies. Abnormality is evil. Disability is the manifestation of evil. These people, these lower class things, have the seal of Satan upon them. From the

The Beast of Bodmin Moor

moment of their birth they are destined to burn in the fiery pits of Hell. They will choke on the sulphurous fumes. Their flesh will melt in the white-hot flames of retribution. For allowing Satan into their bodies, this punishment will be meted out to them. They must suffer so that we [PAUSE] we the strong, the armies of God, the Hammer of Justice can be truly accepted into Heaven. [LONG PAUSE] Erm, let us not forget that it was Satan who caused us to be sent out of the Garden of Eden. That beautiful Utopia, the arena of perfection was given to us by our forgiving God, yet Satan fornicated with Eve and forced her to submit her right to Eden. Adam, like the sheep he was, took himself and his wife out of Eden, and we, his descendants were forced out with him. Because of The Evil One we live in a dystopia, a place ruled by science. Science is Evil. It corrupts. It destroys. Like Satan it promises much, yet returns nothing.

If you are tempted by the Dark One, you MUST resist. You must not give in to the charming guile and the promises of the ultimate sadist. Your fears will become manifest if you do. If you give in to the propaganda and the lies of that [PAUSE] disgusting abomination, your souls will burn in Hell. Set yourself free by laughing in the face of adversity. Do NOT allow your body to be invaded by the hordes of evil. Do NOT relinquish your virginity to an unknown man. You <u>will</u> be copulating with the devil, and you will become the carrier of demon spawn, if you do. You <u>WILL</u> be laid on a table and raped by the Devil. Your wrists will be SLIT and your blood drained. Do you want to sit by Satan in the cauldron of evil? NO!

Release society from the indecencies and depredation brought about by this [PAUSE] No, I am sorry, I cannot continue. The evil that walks this earth will destroy you and myself alike, for his power games. He will rip the very flesh from your feeble frame in order to please himself. You will become the plaything of evil. Fight the Good Fight. Destroy Evil. Destroy your fears. Destroy…"

The huge, medieval oak doors at the far end of the church began to glow a deep orange colour. Father Stephen stopped abruptly. The glow disappeared. He shook his head and opened his mouth to speak once again. Suddenly there was a loud rumbling and the ground began to shake. Stephen feared that the church was at the epicenter of an earthquake, but those fears swiftly subsided and others took their place. Within his mind, the vast number of fears he had played musical chairs, each competing to see who would win. Eventually after much stopping and starting of imagined music, one fear won, however before this fear could reach his central nervous system, Stephen noticed tiny cracks appearing in the stone in front of him. In between the tiny cracks he saw an orangey-red light shine. As the cracks widened the

The Beast of Bodmin Moor

light grew brighter. Steam as hot as Hell billowed out from the cracks. Stephen was scared, but he felt that he needed to show his strength in the face of adversity. He owed it to himself.

The ground he was stood upon became riddled with a myriad of cracks of red light. The very air became a sheet of steam, and the flesh on his body seemed to bubble and burn. In front of him a space of earth six foot by three foot collapsed into the light underneath. Stephen could now see the seething red and white-hot liquid. The ground below him ceased to heave. Aside from his rectangle of lava before him, the church looked pretty much as it had done before: dark, dull, drab, uninspiring.

The patch seemed to take on a hellish tinge. The smell of fire and brimstone attacked his nostrils, invading his air. Stephen found himself struggling to breathe. Fighting for air, he thought that he was hallucinating. As he watched, a head bobbed to the surface of the lava. The horns on the side of the head frightened Stephen. He had read, many times, the story that Jesus told of the Temptation In The Wilderness, and knew off by heart the description that had been given of the Devil, but had just assumed that it was simply another fable created by the Church to fool their congregations. He now knew that he was wrong to have assumed this. He suddenly accepted that Satan was real, and that he was stupid to have ignored the possibility of this reality.

The head began to grow into a full torso, neck and head. As the figure fully emerged from the searing juice of the earth which swiftly scabbed over and healed, Stephen saw nakedness. He had been taught never to look at a man below the waist, but his eyes were now rooted upon the man's genitalia: erect, large, purple, throbbing. With each surging throb of the penis, Stephen's head pounded; a powerful thump which made him want to throw himself into the fiery liquid, from which this ghoul had appeared.

Taking his eyes away from the huge erection, Stephen looked into the creature's eyes. He almost fainted. Blue, piercing light shone from the sockets which contained the man's eyeballs. Not lumps of jelly, but fire. Not even the paltry fire of humans, but that of God. Stephen knew this being for what he was: an angel. He even knew the angel's name: Lucifer, the Light Bringer. The Fallen Angel. The Horned One, Satan, stood before him in all his unholy glory. The fires of Hell had not burnt out the ethereality of the angel's eyes. The light, which was surrounded by blood-red skin and flesh, seemed to bore into Stephen's soul. It seemed to challenge him, to question his faith.

"What do you want of me, O Evil One?" he demanded.

The Beast of Bodmin Moor

The demon stared at Stephen, sheer hatred resting in its eyes. It opened its vast, tooth-filled mouth and spoke. The depth and hollowness of its voice astounded him more than the creature's actual words. The voice seemed to have been echoing through the chambers of Hell for countless aeons. It was a voice made up of the screams of countless tortured individuals, whose torture was immeasurably painful.

"I may be what you consider to be evil, you pompous pile of pig excrement, but nevertheless I demand respect. You will show me this respect, or you will die in the most painful, degrading way that my tortured soul can devise. Just remember to whom you are speaking: the Master of Torture and Pain."

With misplaced bravery, Stephen repeated his demand for the demon's intentions.

"You do not appear to be listening, feeble man. I will kill anyone who upsets me, or at the very least, attempts to do so. Over your numerous years as a priest I have worn the illusion of a parishioner and sat in this church listening to your sermons, and most of them have come very close to securing my wrath, however I have held myself back. Your most recent sermon however is one which I cannot forgive!" the demonic creature bellowed, its breath melting the hairs above Stephen's lip.

Stephen knew that he was going to die, yet he managed to pull himself together in order to demonstrate a level of courage which he did not feel.

"On your knees, vermin!" Stephen commanded, surprising himself with the ferocity of his words.

The demon looked at Stephen quizzically, then slammed his taloned fist straight into Stephen's nose, shattering it. Despite the intensity of the pain, Stephen realised that this was simply a warning. He had been very stupid.

"Even now you still fail to appreciate how much power I have at my fingertips. People in this village will continue to die as a direct result of your insolence. Believe me when I say to you that their deaths, like yours, will be extremely painful and very, very slow." The devil commented, almost matter-of-factly.

Stephen pleaded for forgiveness, but it was to no avail. The demon stuck two, twisted fingers into its own mouth and pushed them deeper and deeper. It began to convulse and from its stomach flowed a cocktail of gory substances: blood, maggots, mould-ridden meat, the finger of a new-born baby and both halves of an illegally

The Beast of Bodmin Moor

aborted baby. Stephen felt extremely nauseous, but managed to ask one important question. Before he died, he wanted to know why. The creature had told him a reason, yet he suspected that there was something that he had not been told. The barbaric creature snarled at him and spoke once more.

"Since long before the time of your religion's idol, Jesus, the name of Satan has been tarnished. All over the world people blame me for all sorts of things – you know the sort of thing I am blamed for, because you speak those lies yourself." The demon paced around the room, waving its incredibly sharp claws through the air, and as it moved about, Stephen found himself searching for the nearest exit. It was too far away to guarantee safety. Before he could have gotten anywhere, the evil creature would have been upon him. He was trapped, and he was forced to listen to the monologue of the Devil.

"Harvest poor this year? Satan's fault. Unable to achieve an erection? Satan is playing with your mind. It is raining? Satan again. Is there nothing that you feeble creatures can find to blame <u>God</u> for? Let me tell you of a few things that your Beloved God has given to you, and blamed me for: tornadoes, disability, nuclear weapons, decreased fertility. You see there was a time long ago when your God was all-powerful. When he wanted to wipe out a race, he could do so with the blink of an eye –

the click of his fingers. Now his powers are much weaker, in fact my powers have grown stronger, because I have not wasted them like your God. Your loving, all-forgiving, all-powerful God wishes to destroy your species, but he no longer has the power to do so. Despite this he is very clever; he knows about horses and riverbanks. If you can take a horse to a riverbank, you cannot make it drink, however if you take that same horse to the same riverbank and hold its head under the water, it will drink as it gasps for air! Of course, it will drown in the process, but who cares?!

And now, oh deluded one, you will go to Heaven, or Hell, and wherever you go, you will be pursued by the ghosts of my words. You will never know whether what I have said is true or not, no matter how much St Peter tries to convince you otherwise. What I have told you is true, but quite frankly I do not care whether you believe me or not."

The frightening, evil demon walked up close to Stephen. With a tongue the texture of coarse sandpaper, it licked his face. Then it thrust its gnarled kneecap deep into Stephen's groin. He feel to the ground, clearly in pain.

"Open your mouth," the demon commanded, and against his will and strength, he found his jaw slacken and his mouth opened wide. He tried to reclose his mouth, but an invisible force which felt like a clamp held it open. The abomination reached down to the ground and scooped up a handful of its own bloody vomit. He poured it into Stephen's mouth and ordered him to swallow. Against his will, the offensive meal forced itself down his throat. As it hit his stomach, Stephen felt an intense pain spread throughout the lower part of his body. He felt as if a fish hook had speared one of his testicles and was trying to rip it in half. The pain began to manifest itself as a light. This bright, white light consumed his sight, and he became blind.

The demon began to laugh which made Stephen even more afraid. His heart was racing, pounding, beating so hard it was almost bursting out of his chest. His skin began to tingle with fear, and sweat dribbled down his back. Suddenly his sight returned but the light had not disappeared. It seemed to envelope the creature in front of him, giving it an eerie, haunting perspective. The red skin of the entity began to crack and melt, as if it were being burnt alive. Mesmerised he watched the flesh blacken and burn. As he looked on, he began to feel the heat on his face. He backed away, attempting to escape the invisible fire.

Suddenly flames licked the monster's pubic hair, and red tongues travelled a circuitous journey up to its head. The creature lifted its head up, and looked deep into Stephen's eyes. Once again he was forced to gaze with awe and wonder at the eyes of an angel. The power contained within those orbs rooted O'Shea to the spot. He found himself unable to speak, or move at all. He wanted to scream his terror and shout his love for the angel of death, but he was still paralysed as the creature moved towards him.

The intense heat that was contained within the body of the demon began to manifest itself physically throughout the church, and Stephen's cassock ignited. The flames quickly consumed his body and the pain he experienced escalated into the highest echelon.

Consumed by the fire, pain and heat his sphincter muscles relaxed and his bowels voided. The excrement in his briefs bubbled and charred in the fires of damnation, and boiling tears rolled from the melting flesh around his eyes.

Stephen was unable to die. He was being kept alive by the demon, who wanted him to feel the pain. It wanted him to realise that God had truly forsaken his servant and his species, but Stephen would not accept the lies of the Devil. He wanted to scream and plead to God, to pray for help and forgiveness for his sins, but the presence of this evil one stopped him. Mentally he was silent. Physically he was still.

The Beast of Bodmin Moor

All was quiet, except for the distinct sound of human flesh cracking within the eternal fires of Hell. And then, out of the silence, came the sounds of Hell itself. Torturous shrieks of pain and suffering invaded his senses, and he became a part of those sounds. He began to see images floating about in the fire; perhaps they were visions of his own personal Hell. He saw the toys of demons, the implements of torture which had been created for the sole purpose of tormenting the unrighteous. The world of human existence had invented many instruments of torture but these paled into insignificance when compared with these butcher-like blades and flesh-twisting spikes. Like a tourist in an under-developed country he empathised and almost felt their pain, yet he could do nothing to help. He felt powerless. He was.

The demon gave him the power to speak his last words on this world. Father Stephen Ray Kieran O'Shea lifted his molten skull up to the heavens and screamed as loudly and as angrily as his broken, smoke-damaged voice box could manage, "My God, my God, why have you forsaken me?"

He fell to the hard, stone floor of the nave and the church burned. The fire of damnation and retribution swept its length, destroying the core of each religious artefact it found. It spread out from the very centre of the icons, drawing out the power and faith that thousands upon thousands of churchgoers had laid upon them over the years. When every religious object had been systematically destroyed, the fire went about destroying the building itself. The demonic beast leapt up out of the fire and dove down towards the hard stone. The ground opened up and the creature swam through the pool of lava. As it swam lower and the lower, the stone, church floor returned to its original state. The demon's vomit glowed a deep purple colour and disappeared.

*****

The Beast of Bodmin Moor

Now then Fred, do be a patient little brother. My story is nearly finished. This article here is from today's newspaper and you will find this most interesting. You remember the article that said one of the victim's tobacco had an "unknown substance" in it? This article has the results of the forensic analysis:

The Bodmin Bugle   17 December

Tobacco Analysed

The forensic analysts who have been analysing the tobacco of a victim of The Beast, have uncovered amazing facts. Since the findings have been uncovered, all of the eyewitness' and victims' belongings have been analysed. Every victim and eyewitness was smoking a tobacco imported from a Middle Eastern country, which was found to contain an "hallucinogenic substance". Police spokespersons issued this statement: "In the light of the recent evidence, we have been able to conclude that The Beast is not truly an evil, malicious messenger of Satan, or an escaped savage zoo animal. We now understand that The Beast is, as the late Jack Kerry suggested, a human serial killer. As yet, we do not know who The Beast is,

Nick Newitt

but we are exploring a range of different lines of enquiry. Under the body of Mr Bluegrieb MP we found a pawprint, but we also found a box of matches from a Devonshire hotel by the name of Childhaven. The manager, Mr Fred Child, 42, is currently away on holiday at this time, but we would like to interview him, so that we can eliminate him from our enquiries. We would like to stress that he is not a suspect, however we would like to talk to Mr Child as soon as possible."

*****

The Beast of Bodmin Moor

So Fred, my dearest brother, you now know my secret. Sadly this means that it is time for you to die. Without you, the chain of evidence which links us is broken. I was careless to have dropped the matches when I killed the MP, but we are as careless as our surname suggests. Do you remember what our headteacher used to say? "Once a Child, always a child." I was always clumsy, and dropping things when we were young. I was even more careless than you, brother dear. Since I became The Beast, and The Beast became me, I am rarely careless. With claws and teeth this sharp, I cannot afford to be careless.

The Beast leapt, and in mid air, its claws sprang out. Before it had even reached its victim, The Beast was slashing and clawing the air, as if practicing. The Beast needed no more practice. It needed the Blood.